5-Minute Hero Stories

📖 SCHOLASTIC

Scholastic Children's Books,
Euston House,
24 Eversholt Street,
London NW1 1DB, UK

A division of Scholastic Ltd
London ~ New York ~ Toronto ~ Sydney ~ Auckland
Mexico City ~ New Delhi ~ Hong Kong

First published in the US by Scholastic Inc. as eight separate titles:
Escape from Prison Island 2016
Deep Sea Treasure Dive 2016
Cops, Crocs and Crooks! 2016
Mystery on the LEGO Express 2014
Halloween Rescue! 2013
Follow That Easter Egg! 2016
Stop That train! 2018
Coastguard to the Rescue 2018

This collected edition first published in the UK by Scholastic Ltd, 2019

ISBN 978 1407 19844 6

Printed in China

2 4 6 8 10 9 7 5 3 1

www.scholastic.co.uk

CONTENTS

ESCAPE FROM PRISON ISLAND

Three crooks are ready to escape Prison Island.

It's almost time!

The crooks have been planning their prison break for weeks.

Tonight, the crooks will finally make their escape.

The three crooks ask Sam if he wants to join their escape.

"We could use a strong guy like you!" says the crooks' leader.

"No, thanks," replies Sam. "I'm too busy lifting weights."

The crooks can't wait to get back to LEGO City!

One crook uses a stolen code to open the cell doors.

Another cuts a wire that turns off the prison's lights.

The crooks crawl through a tunnel. They are almost outside in the prison yard.

The prison is dark and quiet. The crooks sneak across the yard to the front gate.

We're outta here!

The crooks hop into a nearby truck. They zoom down the road towards the dock.

Meanwhile, the guards fix the lights.
Then they set off the alarm.

"Hurry up!" shouts a guard. "The crooks
are getting away!"

Part of the road is under construction. The crooks' truck hits a big bump. They smash through the orange cones.

The truck screeches to a stop. Steam comes out of the engine. A tyre pops off the truck and rolls down the hill.

At the dock, the crooks find a dinghy. But all three crooks won't fit aboard. Two crooks hop in and leave their friend behind.

The guards need their own boat.
They radio for backup.

"Uh-oh," says one crook. "We've sprung a leak."
"Look!" cries another. "Are those sharks?"
"And here comes a police boat," adds the leader.

Then they see a hot-air balloon drop from the clouds.

"Sam?" shouts one crook. "You decided to break out, too?"

"We're saved!" says another.

The crooks climb the rope ladder to the balloon's basket.

"Great timing, Sam!" says the leader.

"We're glad you changed your mind," says another crook.

"We'll lose them in the fog," says Sam.

Sam steers the hot-air balloon through the fog. Finally, they spot dry land. Sam lowers the balloon on to the ground.

DEAP SEA TREASURE DIVE

A diver is in his submarine exploring the deep, dark ocean. He is looking for a sunken ship and its treasure. *It sure is spooky down here*, he thinks to himself.

The diver finally finds what he is looking for – the sunken ship.

But as the diver gets closer, he sees something ghostly nearby that scares him. "What's that?" he cries.

The diver doesn't plan to stick around and find out. He returns to the surface and calls to be picked up.

Back at the deep-sea vessel, he tells the rest of his team what he saw.

The crew has a good laugh at the ghost story, and no one else is afraid.

"Put on your gear, team," says the captain. "We're going after that treasure."

The submarines are lowered into the water. Together, the small fleet explores the deep sea.

Their subs are all different sizes. Some only hold one person and some can hold many.

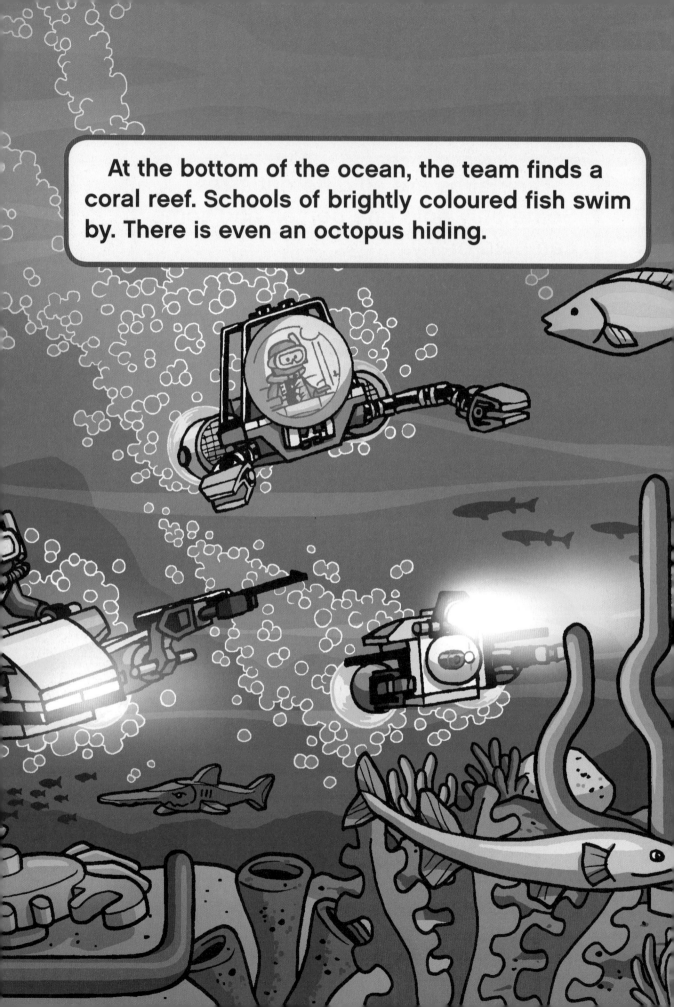

At the bottom of the ocean, the team finds a coral reef. Schools of brightly coloured fish swim by. There is even an octopus hiding.

One diver gets too close to the octopus. The diver is scared. But the octopus is scared of the diver, too!

They both swim away fast. The octopus leaves behind a trail of ink to hide his escape.

The team finds the sunken ship again. They don't see a ghost, but they do see a lot of sharks. It is too dangerous to explore while the sharks are nearby.

The captain has a plan to get those sharks out of there. She radios her ship on the surface for help. "Send down a diver in a shark cage with some bait. That will distract these sharks," she says.

It works! The sharks all swim towards the bait and away from the ship.

The diver spots part of the treasure – a gigantic gem. But he also sees the ghost! It's holding the gem.

The diver wants that gem. But before he can reach for it, the ghost darts away.

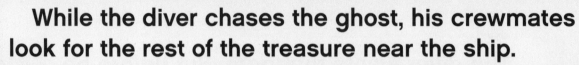

While the diver chases the ghost, his crewmates look for the rest of the treasure near the ship.

First, they use their lights to brighten up the dark ocean floor.

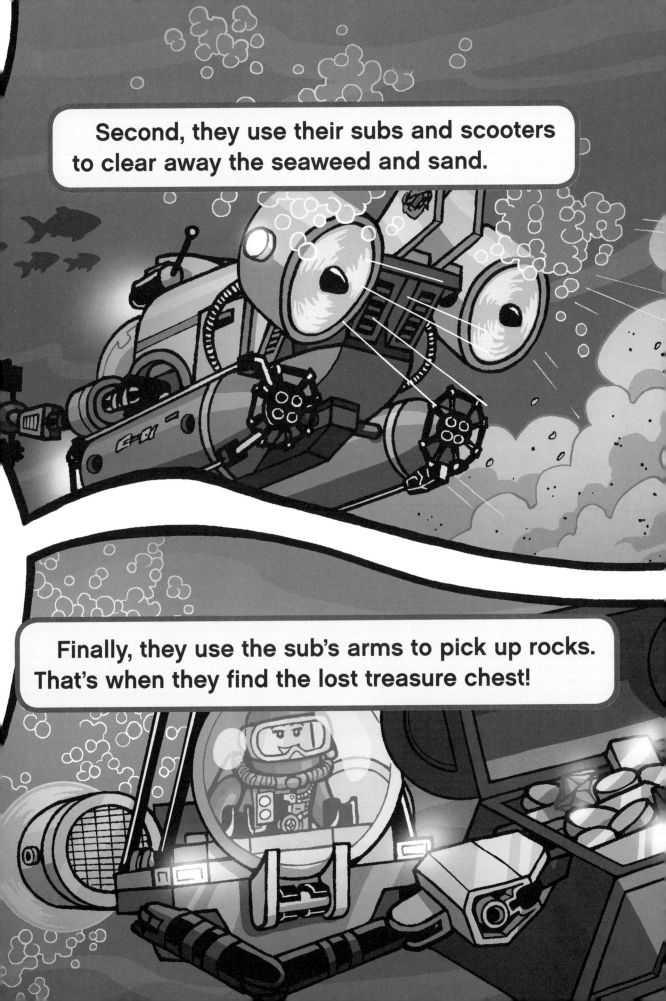

Meanwhile, the diver sees something in a nearby cave. He's scared, but it could be the ghost with that giant gem!

The diver shines his light inside the cave and sees the sparkling gem! It's in the tentacles of a rare white octopus. It wasn't a ghost after all!

Just then, the captain radios, "We found the treasure! Head to the surface."

"I guess we all got some treasure today," the diver says as he swims to the surface.

COPS, CROCS AND CROOKS!

Deep in the swamp, there is a police station. Today they are having a contest to see who will be named 'Swamp Hero'. Everyone from town is invited to watch!

SWAMP HERO CONTEST!

Three police officers will compete in the contest: Carl, Cody and Chloe.

Everyone is so excited that no one notices three crooks nearby. They plan to steal the prize money!

While everyone gets ready for the contest, the thieves take the money.

"Awww, can't we stay and watch?" asks one of the crooks.

"I want to see who wins."

"NO!" the other two hiss.

The bad guys are about to steal a police jeep, but they can't find the keys. Now everyone is heading their way! The crooks have to hide quickly.

The first challenge requires strength. Cody can barely lift up a snake. Chloe lifts an officer over her head.

Carl is the clear winner – he lifts an entire rock over his head! Lucky for the crooks, no one sees them hiding nearby.

"Did you see how strong Carl is? I think he'll win for sure!" says one of the crooks after the crowd is gone. But the others aren't listening. They're too busy fighting over how they almost got caught. They have to be more careful.

The crooks find a boat to steal, but it's out of gas. Suddenly, the judge and contestants are heading this way. The crooks need to hide again!

The next challenge is to see who can build the best boat. Carl builds a raft made of wood. Chloe makes a small airboat.

But Cody wins. He made a super-cool jet boat! The crooks get lucky again and no one spots them hiding in the swamp – no one except a crocodile!

"Did you see how clever Cody was? I bet he'll win!" says one of the crooks. But the others are upset. They almost got caught again! It's time to make a new getaway plan.

The next challenge is to see who can tame the wild crocodiles.

Carl is not a fan of things with scales. Cody is not a fan of things with tails. But Chloe doesn't mind either of those things.

In fact, Chloe *likes* reptiles. And they like her, too. Now the judge doesn't know who should win... There were three challenges and each officer won once. It looks like a three-way tie!

But when the judge goes to get the prize money, he finds that it has been stolen!

Chloe hops from one croc to the next to cross the swamp.

Then, she hops in her boat and grabs a rope. She spins it and throws it.

The hook catches on to the helicopter. The crooks can't get away! But how will Chloe get the crooks down?

With help, of course! Cody and Carl use the police jeep to help pull the crooks down out of the sky.

The judge decides that since Chloe is clever, strong, creative *and* caught the crooks, she deserves to win.

"Chloe, I'm so glad you won!" one of the crooks says with a smile. "I knew you were going to win all along!"

MYSTERY ON THE LEGO EXPRESS

"Please hurry!" Mr Clue says to the taxi driver. He doesn't want to be late for his train. Today he is going on a much-needed holiday.

Mr Clue runs through the train station. His mouth waters when he smells the yummy food nearby. But there's no time for food – he needs to get on that train!

"Whew!" Mr Clue sighs. He made it to the train *just* in time. The whistle sounds as the train pulls out of the station. His holiday has officially started and it's time to relax. But as he closes his eyes to take a nap...

"I can help," says Mr Clue.
"I am the famous actress Marilyn Money, and someone has stolen my golden award statue!" the woman cries.
"I see. Please tell me everything," says the clever detective.

"I was looking out the window at the beautiful view. When I turned around, my acting award statue was gone!" the actress explains. "Someone in this train carriage must have stolen it!"

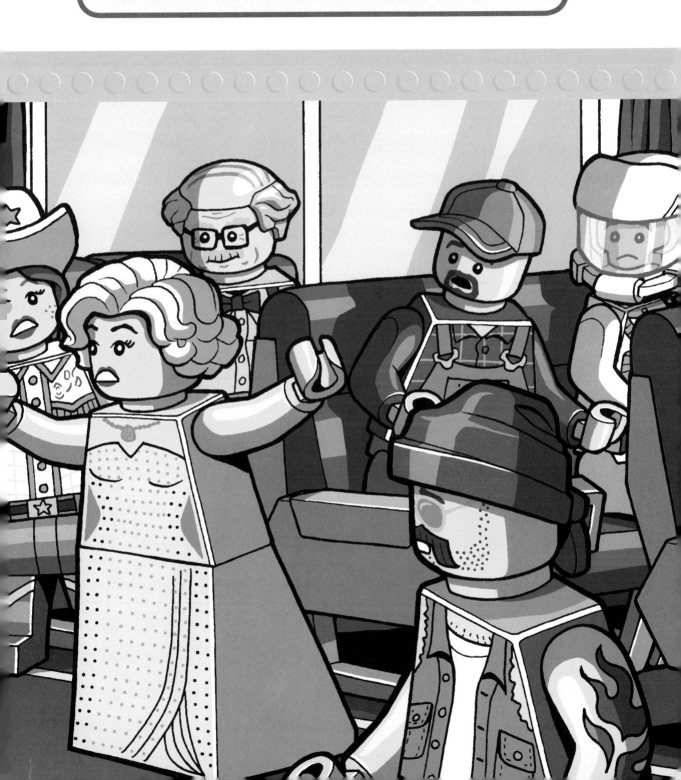

"It wasn't me!" the boxer growls. "I bet *you* did it!"

"No way!" the cowgirl yells. "It was probably *him*!"

Everyone is arguing and pointing at one another. Mr Clue had better solve this crime quickly before people get really upset.

While all of the passengers are fighting, Mr Clue gets to work. He uses his magnifying glass to check the scene of the crime. The actress's seat offers a lot of clues.

"Every person in this train carriage left something at the scene of the crime. It would seem that *ALL* of you are suspects," says Mr Clue. "So, tell me, why were each of you near the gold award?"

I thought the award was one of my gold teeth. Then I remembered my gold teeth are *in* my mouth.

I would never steal anything – except maybe a pony!

It was so pretty, I just wanted to hold it for a minute. But I put it back when I was done.

I was just comparing her award to my trophy, and mine is bigger! Football rules!

91

"But if all of you are innocent, then that leaves only *one* suspect," says Mr Clue. "Where is the *farmer*?"

Everyone turns just in time to see the farmer exit the train carriage.

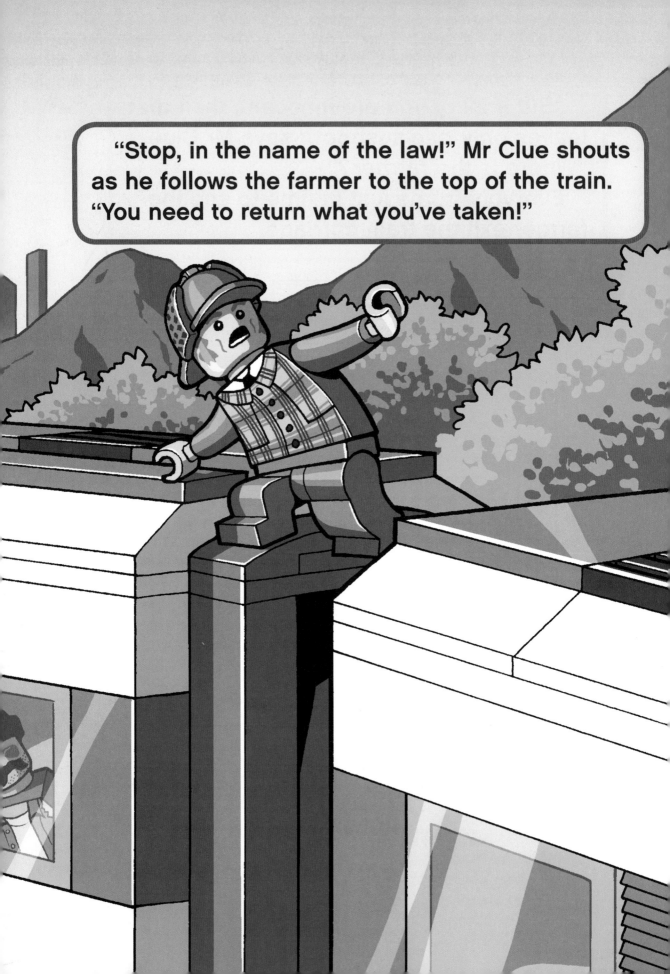

"Stop, in the name of the law!" Mr Clue shouts as he follows the farmer to the top of the train. "You need to return what you've taken!"

The wind and train are so loud, the farmer doesn't hear the detective.

The detective sneaks up behind the farmer before shouting, "You are under arrest, thief!"
"Huh?" says the farmer, startled.
He accidentally squirts milk into Mr Clue's face.

"Sorry about that, mister!" the farmer says. "I came out here to milk my cows. I thought some cookies and milk would help everyone calm down. Did you ever find that award?"

"You mean *you* don't have it?" asks Mr Clue. "Then, where is it?"

Inside the train carriage, Marilyn Money looks inside her handbag. *"Uh-oh!"* she says. "It appears the award was in my bag this whole time."

"It looks like you owe *all* of us an apology!" demands the detective, covered in milk. The other passengers nod their heads in agreement.

Now that the crime has been solved and all the excitement is over, Mr Clue can finally take his nap and start his well-deserved holiday.

HALLOWEEN RESCUE

It is Halloween in LEGO City! The fire service is having a fancy dress party at their new station!

There are so many colourful and fun costumes to wear in LEGO City. Even the fire station's Dalmatian is dressed up.

"Bob and Andy! Those are such great costumes. So lifelike!" the chief says, dressed in a gorilla suit. "Could you help get some more ice for the party?"
"Sure," says Andy, dressed as a monster.
"Of course," says Bob, dressed as a werewolf.

Everyone at the party is having so much fun they don't notice a couple of uninvited guests slip in the back door.

RING-A-RING-A-RING-A-RING! Suddenly, the fire alarm sounds! Everyone jumps into action.

"Bob, Andy, why are you standing around?" the fire chief asks the Monster and Werewolf. "We've got to go!"

The firefighters put on their uniforms. Then they take their places on the fire engine.

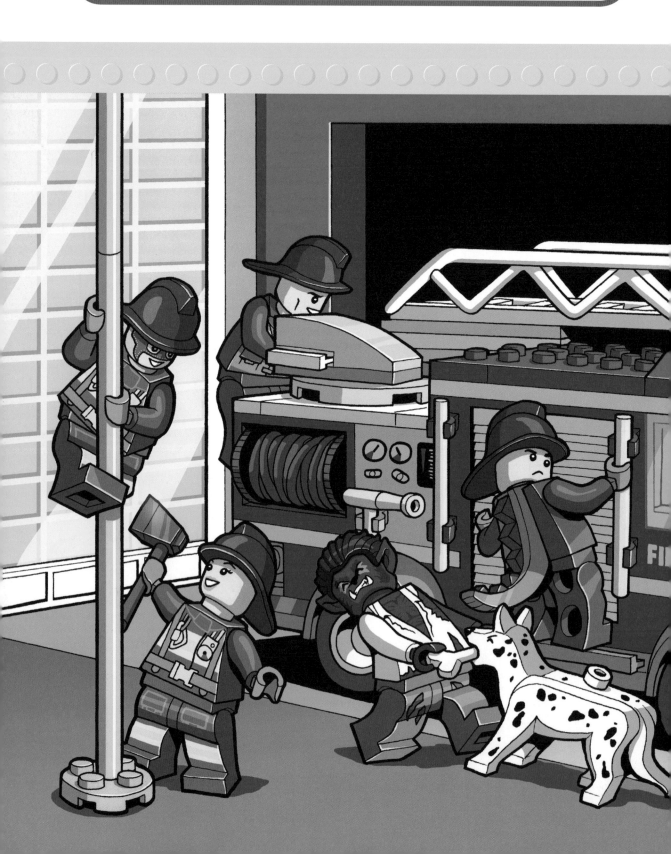

"Stop messing around!" the chief says to the Monster. "We have a fire to put out!"

"*Mmmmrrrrrr*," says the Monster.

The firefighters speed off on their engine to put out the fire. They never know what to expect, but they always do their best!

"We're back with more ice!" says the *real* Andy.
"Hey! You can't leave without us!" says the *real* Bob.
"Wait a minute – if we're here, then *who* is on the fire engine in our place?" asks Andy.

The firefighters arrive at an abandoned house that is on fire. Luckily, no one is in the house. The team works together quickly to put out the fire.

First they extend the ladder, then they pull out the hose and begin to spray water from above.

On the street, the chief and the Monster hold the hose steady to spray the fire from below.

The firefighters use an axe and chainsaw to cut through the front door.

Now the other firefighters can go inside and put out the last of the flames with fire extinguishers.

The fire chief is proud of his team. "A job well done, everyone," he says.

The Monster helped the fire service put out a fire, but the Werewolf has other things on its mind.

"Fire Chief," says a little girl, "can you help get my cat out of that tree?"
"Of course," says the chief.

"Look at Bob eat that fish! He knows how to stay in character," the chief jokes. "*Grrrrr!*" says the Werewolf.

"Andy, you're doing a great job pretending to be a scary monster, too," says the chief.

"*Mmmmrrrrrr*," says the Monster.

Just then, the *real* Bob and Andy drive up to the scene.

"We're so sorry to let you down, sir," Andy says to the fire chief. "We were getting ice when the alarm sounded."

"Who helped you put out the fire?" asks Bob.

"Bob? Andy? I thought *you* were in the monster and werewolf costumes," says the chief.

"Nope," Bob says. "That wasn't us."

The fire chief looks confused. "But if you weren't here, then who helped us?"

The Werewolf and Monster rejoin their friends. "How was your night?" asks the Vampire. "*Mmmmrrrrrr!*" says the Monster. "*Grrrrrr!*" says the Werewolf. "Sounds like the best Halloween ever!" says the Witch.

FOLLOW THAT EASTER EGG!

It is a quiet morning in LEGO City ... until the sound of a security alarm rings out! Barry is breaking his friend Larry out of jail!

The crooks lift a manhole cover. They are about to escape into the sewers. "Yuck, that smells!" says Larry. "I think I'd rather go back to prison!"

"Come on!" yells Barry.

Later, Larry and Barry arrive at their hideout. "I remember this place being nicer," says Larry. "It's no fancy hotel, but it's a great place to hide from the cops," Barry explains.

"I want a nap," says Larry with a yawn.
"We don't have time for naps," snaps Barry. He unrolls a large piece of paper with his plan drawn in crayon.

"Today is Easter and this plan to steal a golden egg is going to make *me* rich!"
"Don't you mean, make *us* rich?" asks Larry.
"Oh, yeah … I meant *us*," says Barry.

Across town, the police chief gives two new cops their first job. "Ryan and Katie, today you'll be driving the armoured car from the bank to the museum."

"We're ready for the challenge, sir," says Katie. "You better bring Reno, the police dog," says the police chief. "You're guarding a priceless treasure." "Yes, sir!" says Ryan.

Ryan and Katie don't get far before they have to stop. A traffic light is lying in the middle of the street.

"Why would someone put a traffic light in the middle of the road on purpose?" asks Ryan.

"I don't know, but Reno thinks this smells fishy," says Katie.

While the police are distracted, Larry and Barry break into the armoured car. "What a beauty!" says Barry. "With this golden egg, *I'm* going to be rich!"

"Don't you mean, *we* are going to be rich?" asks Larry.

"Oh, yeah … *We* are going to be rich," says Barry.

Reno sees Larry and Barry and barks! Ryan and Katie turn to see the crooks making their getaway.

"After them!" shouts Katie.

"Let's hide in that crowd!" says Barry. The two crooks run into the city park. A huge Easter festival is taking place. Everyone is celebrating with games, snacks and lots of painted eggs!

Barry trips and the golden egg flies into the air. It bounces from one balloon to another. "Follow that egg!" Barry shouts to Larry.

The golden egg lands in a bucket of popcorn. "Yay! I haven't eaten since prison," says Larry. "We're not here for a snack, we're here for the golden egg," Barry says.

As soon as Barry gets the popcorn, a bird flies down and grabs the egg.

"That bird is a thief!" Barry shouts as the bird flies away.

"So are you," Larry says. "Maybe you're related."

The mummy bird flies to her nest high in a tree.

"Maybe she thinks the golden egg is one of hers," says Larry. "How cute!"

"It's not cute!" shouts Barry. "She's stealing what we stole first!"

Barry climbs the tree. But the popcorn butter makes the egg slippery. The egg falls through his fingers!

"*My* egg!" shouts Barry.

"Don't you mean, *our* egg?" asks Larry.

Larry tries to catch the golden egg, but it is too slippery. It bounces from his hands to a sign and then off a man's head. It finally lands in a giant pile of golden, chocolate eggs.

EASTER FESTIVAL

"A whole pile of golden eggs!" says Barry. "We are going to be rich!"

"Those aren't *real* golden eggs," says a little girl. "Those are chocolate eggs wrapped in gold foil."

"How are we going to figure out which one is the real egg?" asks Larry.

"Let's eat them!" Barry says.

"What a delicious search!" shouts Larry.

"You better slow down or you'll get a tummy ache," says the little girl.

"*Ouch*!" Barry shouts. One of his teeth breaks when he tries to bite the real golden egg.

"You found it!" says Larry.

"And *we* found *you*!" says Officer Katie.

"Does your jail have a dentist?" asks Barry.

"It sure does." Ryan laughs.

"We captured the crooks, saved the golden egg and got free chocolate," says Katie. "What *sweet* success!"

STOP THAT TRAIN!

One day, a young man rushes through LEGO City to catch his train.

The trains in LEGO City always run on time. Usually that's a good thing – but not today! If he's late to the station, his train might leave without him.

Nothing is going to get in his way – not even the delicious smells coming from the pizza truck. There's no time for pepperoni today!

It's peak travel time in LEGO City. Everyone is getting out of work and ready to have fun – or go home and change into their fuzzy slippers.

A driver for a passenger train watches the clock. He makes sure that travel runs smoothly. "All aboard!" he announces at five o'clock sharp. The train pulls away from the station.

"Wait!" the man yells, but it's too late!

Just outside the station there is a cargo train about to leave. It's heading in the same direction that the man wants to go!

The man runs over and flags down the driver. "Please, I missed my train and I need to get somewhere right away," the man says. "Can I get a ride with you?"

The driver nods. "Okay, but you'll have to ride with the crew."

The crew does not look thrilled at having to fit one more.

As the cargo train leaves the station, the man checks his watch. Everything is back on track ...

... until a farmer and his pigs are blocking the way!
"Can you please move along?" the man shouts.
"Sorry," says the farmer. "I've been trying to get
them to come back to the farm for twenty minutes.
Guess I'm not great at bringing home the bacon!"

Once the pigs are finally gone, the cargo train chugs on its way again. The man and the workers cheer as they make up time by zooming along the tracks.

But then there is a loud crash! The logs on the train have come loose. They are rolling away!

"Whoops!" says the driver as the train slows to a stop. "We can't leave without those logs. Crew, it's time to get that wood out of the woods and back on board!"

"You don't have to tell us twice!" says the crew as they leap into action.

The man can tell that he's going to be late if he doesn't do something now. He finds a pair of binoculars and spots the passenger train from earlier stopped at a station off in the distance!

It's now or never. He runs as fast as he can towards the station. He makes it on the train just as the doors close behind him and waves his ticket in the air. "I made it! I made it!" he cheers and everybody claps.

The man takes the last open seat. Phew! It isn't long before the driver makes an announcement. "Ladies and gentlemen, we have reached our final destination. Thank you for riding with us."

The man leaves the station and rushes to a nearby house, hoping that he isn't too late. The house is dark and it looks like no one is home. He opens the front door.

"SURPRISE!"
A bright light turns on and a crowd of people suddenly jump out from behind doorways and furniture, shouting and waving their arms.

He made it to the surprise party on time! But the surprise isn't for him. He turns off the lights and everyone hides again, waiting for the real guest of honour.

A minute later, the real birthday girl comes home to a big surprise. She can't believe that all her friends remembered her birthday and brought her presents! Well, *almost* all her friends brought her a present.

"I promise I had a present for you," the man tells his friend. "Let's just say your birthday gift is that I even made it to this party at all!"

COASTGUARD TO THE RESCUE

"Good morning, LEGO City, and thanks for tuning in to today's weather report! We've got a beautiful day ahead of us: sunny with a chance of WOW! So don't waste the day staying inside. It's time for some fun in the sun!"

No one in LEGO City ever misses the morning weather report. Everyone is ready for a bright and perfect day.

A surfer dude heads out to catch some waves. Jet Skiers are totally ready to race across the water. A scuba diver can't wait to explore under the sea.

"And we're clear," says the camerawoman. "Great job, everyone!"
With the weather report over, the weatherman decides to enjoy the day, too. He's going to take his brand-new sailboat, *Sunny Side Up*, out for a ride.

With so many people visiting the water, the LEGO City coastguard is on patrol. The coastguard's job is to make sure everyone has a safe and fun day.

The warm weather is so peaceful that no one is in danger – so even the coastguard crew has time for a little rest and relaxation.

A little fishing, a little game of Go Fish and a little yoga make the crew healthy, stealthy, and wise.

But then there is something strange on the horizon. Grey storm clouds start rolling in fast. The waves in the water become choppy.

The crew quickly jumps into action. Here comes the coastguard to the rescue!

The boat navigates through the wild waters to help the Jet Skiers first. The crew members act fast. They use the spotlight to find the skiers. Then they throw lifebelts to pull the skiers back to safety.

The captain realizes that the storm is too big for one ship to handle the rescue on its own. It is time to call for reinforcements.

There is a rumble in the sky. It's a coastguard aeroplane swooping in! It will save the surfer before the strong tide pulls him into the open water.

"Dude, am I ever so pumped to see you!" cheers the surfer. "These waves are too gnarly to hang ten!"

Further out, a coastguard helicopter spots the scuba diver. A rescue diver is lowered into the water on a hook to save the diver.

"This must be what a fish feels like!" says the scuba diver. "You caught me hook, line and sinker!"

There is still someone else who needs the coastguard's help. It's the weatherman! He tries to control his sailing boat as it rocks

back and forth in the wind. But he has bigger problems as he looks out at the ocean. "Oh, no. It appears to be cloudy with a hundred per cent chance of ... SHARKS!"

The weatherman finds a flare and fires it into the sky. A bright burst of light tells the coastguard exactly where he is.

But the waves are getting higher and the shark is getting closer.

Suddenly, the shark swims alongside the boat. The shark pushes it carefully through the waves toward a small island! "Whoa! You don't want to eat me. You want to save me!" the weatherman exclaims.

Once they reach the island, the weatherman leaps from the boat and waves to the shark. "That was a fin-tastic rescue!" yells the weatherman as the shark swims back into the ocean.

The coastguard helicopter lands on the island to pick up the stranded weatherman. One of the rescuers says, "We're glad you're okay, sir. But what happened to your weather prediction?"

Suddenly, the rain clears, the water calms down, and the sun starts to peek through the clouds.

The weatherman shrugs and smiles. "I said it would be sunny today. I just didn't say *how much* of the day would be sunny."

Luckily for LEGO City, the coastguard is always ready to protect and serve – even on the sunniest days.

THE END!